The Pirates' Picnic

Other Early Readers
by Angela McAllister

Sophie's Dance Class

The Pirates' Picnic

Angela McAllister

Illustrated by
Giulia Orecchia

Orion
Children's Books

First published in Great Britain in 2014
by Orion Children's Books
This edition published in 2016 by Hodder and Stoughton

5 7 9 10 8 6

A CIP catalogue record for this book
is available from the British Library.

ISBN 978 1 4440 1094 7

Printed and bound in China

The paper and board used in this book are
made from wood from responsible sources.

Orion Children's Books
An imprint of
Hachette Children's Group
Part of Hodder and Stoughton
Carmelite House
50 Victoria Embankment
London EC4Y 0DZ

An Hachette UK Company
www.hachette.co.uk

www.orionchildrensbooks.co.uk

For Luke by the salty sea.
Hope you never have to
eat a beak pasty!

Contents

Chapter One

The pirates of the bad ship Skullywag were fed up. They hadn't found any treasure for weeks.

"We're no good," moaned
Lanky Lou.

"We're useless," groaned
Bristly Bert.

"We're rubbish," grumbled
Grumpy Greg.

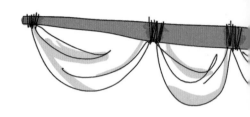

Jim the cabin boy looked
around the deck.

The sails were saggy.

The mop was droopy.

Even the Jolly Roger looked
glum.

"I thought being a pirate was supposed to be fun," Jim said to Rotter, his pet rat.

He went to see Captain Bold.

"I don't know what to do,
Jim," said the Captain. "Pirates
need to find treasure and have
adventures. What can we do to
cheer up the crew?"

"We could hunt for treasure?"
said Jim.

"No," sighed the Captain.
"A rat ate the map."

"We could dance the hornpipe?" said Jim.

"No," sighed the Captain. "A rat ate the fiddle strings."

"We could have a swim?"
said Jim.

"No," sighed the Captain.
"A rat ate the rubber rings."

Then Jim remembered how his mother used to cheer him up.

"We could have a picnic?" he said.

Captain Bold smiled. "I love picnics," he said. "That's the way to cheer up a gloomy crew. Well done, Jim lad."

Chapter Two

Captain Bold called all the pirates on deck.

"Cheer up, boys," he said. "Jim's had a brilliant idea – we're going to have a picnic!"

"Hurray!" cheered Jim.

"Pack the buckets and spades!" ordered the Captain. And he went to hunt for his sun cream.

But the pirates looked as gloomy as ever.

"What's the matter?" said Jim.
"Don't you like picnics? We've
got a whole day off – no scrubbing
decks or mending sails. We might
even have an adventure!"

"The picnic *is* the problem," said Bristly Bert. "Captain Bold always makes us row for hours to find a perfect beach."

"But at least the sun is shining," said Jim.

"Oh, it won't be for long," said Lanky Lou. "It always rains when we go on a picnic."

"What about playing games?" said Jim. "Isn't that fun?"

"Not really," sighed Grumpy Greg. "We have to let Captain Bold win all the games. It's a pirate's duty to keep the Captain happy."

"Well, what about the food? I *love* picnic food!" said Jim.

"You won't love *pirates'* picnic food," said Bristly Bert. "Last year we had pasties made with lumps of stewed boot and rotten seagull."

"And I got the beak!" said Lanky Lou.

At that moment a disgusting smell floated up from the kitchen.

Oh dear, thought Jim. Maybe a picnic isn't such a good idea after all.

Chapter Three

When the picnic was ready everything was put in the rowing boat.

"Breathe in!"

"Mind your elbow!"

"Watch what you do with that cutlass!"

Jim helped Frazzle the cook aboard.

"Hold this," said Frazzle, and he handed Jim a big glass jar.

"Aaargh!" Jim screamed. "It's full of eyeballs!"

"Those are *eggs*, boy." Frazzle licked his lips. "You can't have a picnic without rotten eggs."

The pirates looked at one another.

"I told you," said Bristly Bert.

"Now, start rowing, lads," said Captain Bold.

"Which way?" asked Jim.

"South is sunny," said Bristly Bert.

"East is nearer," said Grumpy Greg.

"West is best," said Lanky Lou.

"It's my boat," said the Captain,
"and I want to go north!"

The boat rocked from side to
side as the pirates argued.

Just then the boat heaved up
high out of the water.

"Aaargh!!" roared the pirates.

Chapter Four

"Where did the sea go?" cried
Lanky Lou.

"I'm feeling dizzy!" wailed
Bristly Bert.

"Mummy!" cried Grumpy
Greg.

Jim looked over the edge. A huge whale was underneath the boat. It started to swim off fast.

"Hold on tight, everyone," said Jim, laughing. "We've got a lift!"

"I like travelling by whale-power," said Bristly Bert.

For the first time that day, the
pirates began to smile.

Captain Bold pulled out his
telescope to search for an island.

Before long, the Captain shouted, "Tropical island ahoy! I spy the perfect place for a picnic."

"But how do we get off the whale, Captain?" said Lanky Lou.

"Don't make me jump!" cried Bristly Bert.

"I can't swim!" wailed Grumpy Greg.

Jim had an idea. "I'll set us free, Captain," he said.

He pulled Rotter out of his pocket and dangled him over the side of the boat.

"Hold on, everyone!" cried Jim.

Rotter grinned and bit the whale.

With a whoosh, the whale dived under the water and the boat slid back into the sea towards the island.

Chapter Five

The pirates were so busy rowing
to the island that they didn't see
the dark clouds above.

"Hurry up, boys," said Captain Bold. "We'll soon be playing Pirate in the Middle."

Splat! The first raindrop fell in Grumpy Greg's boot.

Splat! The second raindrop fell on Lanky Lou's nose.

Splat! The third raindrop fell on Captain Bold's eyepatch.

"Put up the umbrella!" cried
the Captain.

"Row faster, boys!" he said.
"We must get to the island before
the storm comes."
But it was too late.

Thunder crashed, lightning flashed and down came lots of rain.

Oh dear, thought Jim with a shiver.

Suddenly, a huge wave flung the boat upside down. The pirates were washed ashore, dripping and spluttering.

Chapter Six

The pirates pulled the boat onto
the beach.

"Save the picnic!" cried
Frazzle. But the basket was
already floating away.

Grumpy Greg grinned. "No stewed boot!" he whispered.

Bristly Bert giggled. "No rotten seagull!" he hissed.

Lanky Lou did a little dance. "No beak! Hurray!"

Then, suddenly, they heard the
loud rumble of empty tummies.
"No food at all!" the pirates
gasped.

Everyone was so miserable, they didn't notice Frazzle creep away with the jar of rotten eggs.

"At least the rain has stopped," said Jim. "Let's play some games."

"But we've lost our bats and balls," said Grumpy Greg.

Jim looked around. "We can use sticks and coconuts," he suggested.

Captain Bold started to smile. "Hmm . . . Stick and Coconut," he said. "I expect I'm good at that."

Sure enough, the Captain won
Stick and Coconut.

Then he won
Hunt the Rat.

Then he won Pirate in the
Middle.

Next it was Musical Pirates. "I'm always very good at that," said Captain Bold.

While the Captain put on some sun cream, the pirates huddled together.

"I'm fed up of losing," whispered Bristly Bert.

"Me too," said Grumpy Greg.

"But you told me it's a pirate's duty to keep the Captain happy," said Jim.

Lanky Lou grinned. "It's also a pirate's duty to behave very badly! This time it's each man for himself!"

The game began. Jim whistled the music. When he stopped, all the pirates stood as still as statues.

Suddenly . . .

"Ouch!" A crab nipped Captain Bold on the toe.

Splat! A seagull sat on his head.

Glurp! He began to sink in quicksand!

"Help!" he cried.

None of the pirates moved.

"Get me out!" roared Captain Bold. "That's an order!"

The pirates had to follow an order. They rushed to pull out the Captain.

"Ha ha! I win!" said Captain Bold.

"You tricked us!" they cried.

"It's a pirate's duty to behave very badly!" said Captain Bold.

"That's not fair," moaned Lanky Lou.

"I'm not playing any more," groaned Grumpy Greg.

"Me neither," grumbled Bristly Bert.

The pirates sat sulking silently on the beach. The only sound was the rumbling of their hungry tummies.

Suddenly they noticed Frazzle, sitting on a rock, eating his eggs.

"Maybe rotten eggs aren't so bad," thought Bristly Bert.

"There's nothing else to eat except seaweed," thought Grumpy Greg.

"If I swallow them whole, maybe they won't taste so bad," thought Lanky Lou.

And before you could say, "Yo, ho, ho!" the pirates made a dash for Frazzle.

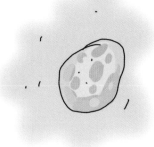

Chapter Seven

Frazzle held the last rotten egg up to his lips and . . .

"Ouf!"

"Ouch!"

"Gerrof!"

A jumble of pirates landed on his lap.

"I've got it!" cried Jim and he snatched the rotten egg out of Frazzle's hand.

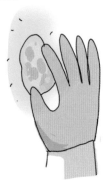

But the egg was slimy. It popped out of Jim's fingers and bounced away down the rocks.

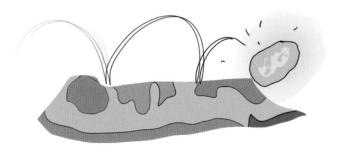

"Run, boys, run," shouted Captain Bold.

The rotten egg rolled over the rocks and dropped into a dark hole.

The pirates stared at the hole.
There was something glinting
inside.

Rotter jumped out of Jim's
pocket and scurried into the hole.
When he peeped out again, he
had a coin in his mouth.

"Treasure!" cried the pirates.

Inside the hole was a chest full of gold and jewels!

"Well done, Jim lad," said Captain Bold. "Your picnic has cheered everyone up and made us rich! You're a fine pirate!"

Jim smiled happily. "And look," he cried. "Food!"

Along the beach was the
Tropical Island Cafe.

The pirates were soon gobbling
down fish and chips and bowls
of ice-cream. They paid with a
big fat ruby.

Everyone agreed that the worst
picnic had turned out to be the
best after all.

"Three cheers for Captain
Bold," said Jim, "and the pirates
of the bad ship Skullywag!"

What are you going to read next?

Have more adventures with Horrid Henry,

and travel the world with Miranda the Explorer.

Play clever tricks with Twit,

spend Mondays at Monster School,

and even brave The Dragon's Dentist . . .

Learn how love is just like a Woolly Hat,

dance under The Little Nut Tree,

take home Monstar, the best pet ever,

and have an extra-special Mr Monkey birthday party!

Enjoy all the Early Readers.